JUN 1998

ANDRES GALARRAGA
THE BIG CAT

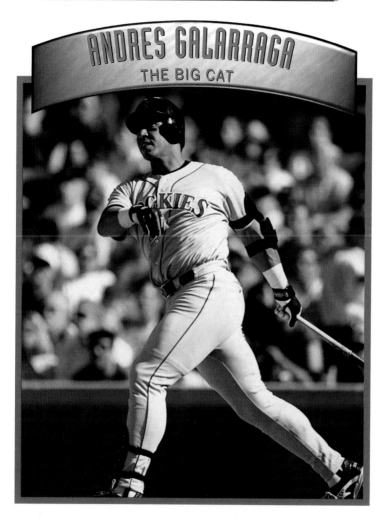

BY MARK STEWART

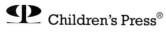 Children's Press®

A Division of Grolier Publishing
New York London Hong Kong Sydney
Danbury, Connecticut

Photo Credits
©: Allsport USA: 31, 37, 45 top right (Stephen Dunn), 35 (Otto Greule Jr.), 40 (Jed Jacobson); AP/Wide World Photos: 8; Daniel Bunch/The Daily Journal: 13; John Klein: cover, 14; Miguel Romero: 15, 44 top left; Ron Vesely: 17, 21, 25, 27, 32, 39, 42, 43, 45 top left, 47; Sporstchrome East/West: 3, 6, 28 (Rob Tringali Jr.), 18, 44 top right, 46; Tom Dipace: 22; UPI/Corbis-Bettmann: 10

Library of Congress Cataloging-in-Publication Data

Stewart, Mark.
    Andres Galarraga : the big cat / Mark Stewart.
        p. cm. —(Sports stars)
        Summary: A biography of the slugger from Venezuela, known as the Big Cat, who won the National League championship for most runs batted in and most home runs in 1996.
        ISBN 0-516-20483-1 (lib. bdg.)   0-516-26048-0 (pbk.)
        1. Galarraga, Andres, 1961- —Juvenile literature. 2. Baseball players—Venezuela—Biography—Juvenile literature. [1. Galarraga, Andres, 1961- . 2. Baseball players.] I. Title. II. Series.
GV865.G25S84   1997
796.357'092   96-40436
[B]—DC21   CIP
                                                AC

★ CONTENTS ★

★ 1 ★

POWER THREAT

Andres Galarraga steps into the batter's box and waits for the next pitch. Andres knows that the pitcher will probably not risk a fastball on the inside portion of the plate. That pitch is Andres's favorite. He can rip it down the line and into the seats for an easy home run. The crowd grows quiet as the pitcher winds up and delivers a nasty breaking pitch. Andres sees the rotation on the ball, judges its location, and begins his swing.

The pitcher had hoped to sneak a ball over the outside part of the plate, but Andres leans into the pitch, extends his arms, and drives the ball the opposite way to the right field wall. By the time the outfielders scramble to throw the ball to the infield, it is too late. Galarraga is safe at second base, flashing a brilliant smile at the cheering crowd.

Baseball was not always this much fun. At one time an All-Star, Andres went into a vicious hitting slump that lasted three years. He heard boos that rocked his confidence and almost drove him from the game. But Andres did not quit. He relearned the fundamentals of hitting and earned the respect of every pitcher in the league.

Andres plays for the Colorado Rockies.

CRAZY ABOUT BASEBALL

Andres Galarraga grew up in the working-class neighborhood of Caracas, a city in Venezuela. From the age of five, baseball was practically all he ever played or talked about. As soon as he met his friends in the morning, Andres started arranging baseball games, even if it was a school day. "I used to get everybody in trouble," laughs Andres. "We would play before school, and sometimes during school instead of going to class. I would say, 'Let's keep playing,' and we would miss class. I just loved the game so much. It's all I wanted to do."

Andres dreamed that he would one day play professional baseball like his hero, Roberto Clemente.

When Andres was not on the baseball diamond, he was watching his favorite players on television. Among the many Venezuelan players in the major leagues during the 1960s and 1970s were All-Stars Luis Aparicio, Dave Concepcion, and Vic Davalillo. Andres also rooted for Puerto Rico's Roberto Clemente, the greatest Latin star of them all. Andres studied everything about the stars—from their hitting and fielding techniques to their quirks and habits. And that's how he learned to play baseball.

Andres's father, Francisco, was a housepainter who had little interest in baseball. But he was pleased that his son was so passionate about something. He supported Andres's interest as best he could. When school was out, Andres went to work painting with his father. But Andres's mind was always somewhere else. "Baseball was all I thought about when I painted," Andres says. "I saw myself hitting home run after home run. I was crazy to play the game."

⭐ ⭐ ⭐

Andres was the youngest of five children. His mother, Juana, liked to spoil him because he was her "baby." She would make huge meals for him whenever he was hungry, and she praised him when he cleaned his plate. Unfortunately, this led to a weight problem. Despite playing sports several hours a day, Andres was just plain fat. When the other children teased him, he felt horrible. Eventually, he found that he could stop their teasing by flashing a big, toothy smile—the smile that is his "trademark" today!

Andres continued to pack on the pounds through his teenage years. But as he grew taller, that extra weight gave him awesome power at the plate. By the time he enrolled at Enrique Felmi High School, everyone had heard about the young man with the incredible home-run stroke. Andres made the school team easily and did not disappoint his fans. In 19 games, he nailed 15 homers. Soon everyone was telling Andres that he was good enough to make the Venezuelan national team.

When teammates teased Andres about his weight, he would respond with a bright smile.

Andres's extra weight gives him tremendous hitting power.

So at the age of 16, Andres tried out. To his astonishment, the coach cut him from the team. Andres went home and cried. He felt he was as good as anyone on the field. Several weeks later, the coach reconsidered and asked Andres to join the team, but Andres refused. Instead, he signed to play for the Caracas Lions, a team that competed in the Venezuelan Winter League. It was the best decision he could possibly have made.

On the Lions, Andres was surrounded by top pros. Among his teammates were Manny Trillo, the All-Star second baseman of the Chicago Cubs, and

Andres developed his pro game while playing on the Caracas Leones.

Tony Armas, who had hit 13 home runs as a
rookie for the Oakland A's that summer. Andres
watched, listened, and learned. "When they did
drills, I did drills," Andres says. "When they ran, I
ran. I watched everything they did. I said, 'This
is what I have to do to be a major leaguer.'"

By the time Andres was 17, he stood over 6
feet tall and weighed more than 250 pounds. His
team's general manager believed Andres already
had the size and talent to make it in the major
leagues—all he needed was some experience in
the minors. He invited Felipe Alou, a scout for
the Montreal Expos, to take a look at the young
star. Alou was impressed. He contacted the Expos
and advised them to sign "the fat kid who hits"
before any more scouts showed up. They took his
advice and in early 1979, Andres became
an Expo.

Andres was signed by the Montreal Expos in 1979.

Andres's power quickly won him the respect of his teammates.

★ 3 ★

ROAD TO THE MAJORS

In March 1979, Andres Galarraga reported to the Montreal Expos spring-training facility—only to hear the same laughter that had haunted him as a youngster in Caracas. Who was this pudgy 18-year-old, his new teammates wondered, an overweight fan? Andres flashed his smile and stepped into the batter's box. He proceeded to launch six home runs in a row and turned to see a bunch of open mouths. No one was laughing at "The Caracas Kid" anymore.

Andres was assigned to the organization's West Palm Beach team in the Florida State League. Being away from home for the first time was very hard for Andres. He didn't know a single word of English, and his performance on the field suffered.

After picking up only three hits in seven games, Andres was demoted. He was sent to the Pioneer League in Calgary. Calgary, a remote city in the Canadian Rockies, is about as far as you can get from Venezuela. "I was completely lost and very scared," Andres recalls. "I wanted to call home every day, but there wasn't enough money for that. It was terrible, really. I couldn't communicate. And it was so different. When I got to Calgary, it was cold and I didn't have a coat or sweaters."

Adjusting to a foreign culture is a big problem for many Latin American players, especially when they come to the United States and Canada as teenagers. Often, they make the move even more difficult by hanging out only with other Latin players. In Calgary, Andres and his Spanish-speaking teammates would go to a

As Andres became more comfortable in North America,
his hitting improved.

From 1982 to 1984, Andres steadily improved his play.

restaurant, point at items on the menu and then wait to see what they had ordered.

In 1981, after two seasons at Calgary, Andres was promoted to Jamestown of the New York–Penn League. When he arrived, he discovered that he was the only Hispanic player on the club. At first, he was terrified. But he soon realized this predicament was actually a blessing. "The best thing for me was going to Jamestown," Andres says. "I was the only Latin player on the team, so it forced me to speak English. I was very lonely there, but I learned the language much quicker. I would read my dictionary, watched a lot of TV, and read the newspapers."

As Andres began to feel more comfortable off the field, his game began to improve. He played first base, third base, catcher, and outfield for Jamestown and batted a respectable .260. He returned to West Palm Beach for the 1982 and 1983 seasons, and he really hit his stride in 1984 for the Expos' Jacksonville affiliate. Andres belted 27 homers that year and finished first in total bases, slugging, putouts, assists, and double plays. For his marvelous efforts, he was named Southern League MVP. The highlight of 1984, however, came before the season even started, when he and his high-school sweetheart, Eneyda, were married.

The Expos had big plans for Andres. He would put in a full season at the AAA level with Indianapolis, then move to the majors in September 1985. By 1986, they hoped he would be ready to win the starting first baseman's job. And that is exactly what happened. Andres put up great numbers and hit awesome home runs that fans are still talking about years later. Andres was so feared that he sometimes drew intentional walks with the bases empty. He also displayed the quickness that would soon earn him the nickname "The Big Cat." In a brief audition with the Expos that fall, he hit a couple of homers and showed flashes of his tremendous defensive ability.

Andres won the starting first baseman's job for the Expos at the beginning of the 1986 season.

★ 4 ★

SUCCESS AND DECLINE

During the spring of 1986, Montreal manager Buck Rodgers insisted that he would not rush Andres Galarraga. But everyone, including Andres, knew that the Expos were counting on him to produce big numbers. Andres was playing well until he injured his knee in July and had to spend nearly two months on the disabled list. He came back for the final three weeks of the season and picked up where he left off, finishing with 10 home runs and a .271 batting average in 105 games.

In 1987, the "injury bug" bit Andres again. A high inside fastball severely bruised the thumb on his right hand—considered the "top hand" for a right-handed power hitter. The intense pain made it impossible for him to whip his bat at pitches and pull the ball down the line. Andres wanted to stay in the lineup, so he adjusted. For the rest of the year, he hammered the ball to the opposite field, defying the scouting reports that said he would try to pull everything. Had the pitchers known that Andres was incapable of

Andres was as talented in the field as he was at the plate.

In the 1988 season, Andres became one of the top hitters in the National League.

pulling the ball, they would have thrown inside all year long instead of laying the ball out over the plate! His .305 average was his best yet as a pro and ranked seventh in the National League (NL). "That made me very confident," Andres remembers. "But I was frustrated because I hit only 13 home runs."

As it turned out, he had nothing to worry about. When the 1988 season began, pitchers could hardly wait to pound Andres inside. Little did they realize that he was now fully recovered from his hand injury. Time and again, they fed fastballs right to Andres's strength, and Andres punished the ball all season long. It was July before his opponents figured out they were pitching him incorrectly, and Andres already had 20 home runs. When they began pitching him outside, he simply used the smooth stroke that had worked so well the year before. The result was 42 doubles and 184 hits—both tops among NL batters.

It seemed that the sky was the limit for Andres. At least the Expos thought so. Believing their young slugger could pump out 35 to 45 homers a year, they asked him to open up his stance so that he could pull more pitches. As always, Andres agreed cheerfully. He did not realize it at the time, but this nearly caused the end of his baseball career. "I had a decent season, but I felt confused at the plate," he says. "I felt like I was losing my natural swing. People started throwing me fastballs inside, and I couldn't get my hands through."

Over the next three seasons, Andres's batting average plummeted nearly 100 points. And the more coaches tinkered with his swing, the worse it got. For the first time as an Expo, Andres was hearing boos. After batting .219 with just nine home runs in 1991, Andres was traded to the St. Louis Cardinals for a promising young pitcher named Ken Hill.

After changing his batting stance, Andres started to struggle at the plate.

Andres hoped to have a good year in St. Louis.

Things only got worse. Prior to spring training, Andres's father passed away. Andres was ashamed that his father had seen him fail to fulfill his potential. And as he battled through a series of minor injuries to keep his average above .200, he heard the boos of the fans once again. To make matters even worse, Ken Hill was having a spectacular year with the Expos. "I never told anybody, not the media, not my teammates, nobody, but I thought about going home, giving up," Andres admits. "I thought about it during the season. I couldn't do anything. I was so down."

Luckily, though Andres had lost faith in his own abilities, there was one person who had not—Cardinals batting coach Don Baylor. He urged Andres not to give up and asked him if he was willing to start learning all over again how to hit. Feeling he had nothing left to lose, Andres said yes.

***

Baylor began by teaching Andres the fundamentals of hitting. He stressed the importance of seeing the ball well and gave Andres a brand-new stance that let him get a better look at the pitcher. Slowly but surely, Andres began to improve, and in the last six weeks of the 1991 season, he batted .301 with eight homers and 29 RBIs.

Cardinals batting coach Don Baylor urged Andres not to give up.

★ 5 ★

TRIUMPHANT COMEBACK

Shortly after the 1992 season ended, Baylor was hired to manage the Colorado Rockies, who were preparing for their first season. When he heard that the Cardinals had chosen to let Andres go as a free agent, Baylor grabbed him. It was the steal of the year. Andres collected two hits on Opening Day and stayed hot all year long.

The combination of Baylor's adjustments, the thin air of Denver, and the return of Andres's confidence produced an incredible season. For much of 1993, Andres's average hovered around .400, and he became the first Colorado player to appear in the All-Star Game. Andres finished the year as the NL batting champion and was

After Don Baylor became manager of the Colorado Rockies, he asked Andres to come play on his team.

Coached by Baylor, Andres started to hit the ball again.

honored as the league's Comeback Player of the Year. His .370 average was the highest for a right-handed hitter since Hall of Famer Joe DiMaggio hit .381 in 1939. Could he have hit .400 if he had the chance to do it all over again?

"I don't think it's impossible, but there's a lot of pressure," Andres says. "You do a lot of media interviews and they always remind you about hitting .400. I tried not to think about it, but sometimes I'd look at the scoreboard and see my average around .400 and I would say, 'I've got to get a hit this time.'"

All of baseball applauded Andres for not giving up. But as far as he is concerned, the credit for his amazing turnaround belonged to someone else. "I'll tell you who I dedicate it all to—Don Baylor," Andres says. "He believed in me, and he worked with me. If it wasn't for him, I'm not here right now."

Since his terrific 1993 season, Andres has only gotten better. He topped the .300 mark again in

Andres enjoyed his first season in Colorado.

1994 and added 31 homers. In 1995, he knocked
in 100 runs for the first time in his career and
led NL first basemen in putouts. In 1996, Andres
went wild at the plate, leading the league in home

After hitting a home run, Andres is congratulated by a teammate.

runs and RBIs. His 150 RBIs set a league record for first basemen, and his 47 home runs were the most by an NL first baseman since 1955.

Today, baseball is fun again for Andres. He plays in a wonderful ballpark in front of great fans, and he commands respect around the league. But it's not just for his high batting average and long home runs. He is a role model on and off the field, especially in Denver, which has a large Hispanic population. The Denver Boys & Girls Club named its baseball field in honor of Andres after he donated money to improve it. Andres makes sure to give his support to good causes in the Denver area because he wants the fans to come out and support him. It should come as no surprise that Andres feels he plays better when the stands are full and the crowd is loud. "In baseball, I thrive on the electricity I get from the fans. The heat, sweat, and emotions—I like it when they get involved."

Andres is a little older and a lot wiser than he was when he first came to the majors, although you might not know it to look at him. He still feels the joy and excitement of a rookie every time he takes the field.

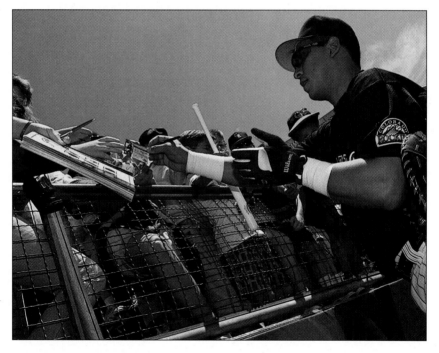

Andres signs autographs for eager fans at Coors Field in Denver.

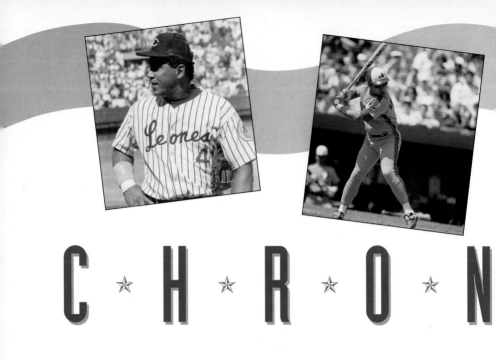

C ★ H ★ R ★ O ★ N

1961	• June 18: Andres Galarraga is born in Caracas, Venezuela.
1979	• Andres signs with the Montreal Expos organization.
1984	• Playing in the minor leagues, Andres is named the MVP of the Southern League.
1985	• Andres is named American Association Rookie of the Year playing for the Expos AAA team in Indianapolis. In September, he makes his major league debut.
1988	• Andres leads the NL in hits and doubles in 1988 and plays in his first All-Star Game. He is named the league's top first baseman by *Baseball America* and *USA Today.*
1989	• Andres wins his first of two consecutive Gold Glove awards as best fielding first baseman in the NL.

O ★ L ★ O ★ G ★ Y

1991 • November 25: Andres is traded to St. Louis Cardinals.

1992 • November 17: After playing one season for
St. Louis, Andres signs with the Colorado Rockies.

1993 • With a .370 average, Andres wins the NL batting
title. Andres also records the first hit in Rockies
history, a single off Dwight Gooden of the Mets
on Opening Day.

1995 • For the first time in his career, Andres knocks in
100 runs.

1996 • Andres is the NL home run and RBI champion. The
last first baseman to accomplish this feat was Hall
of Famer Willie McCovey, who led the league in 1969.

1997 • Andres becomes the all-time home run leader of
Venezuelan major-league baseball players.

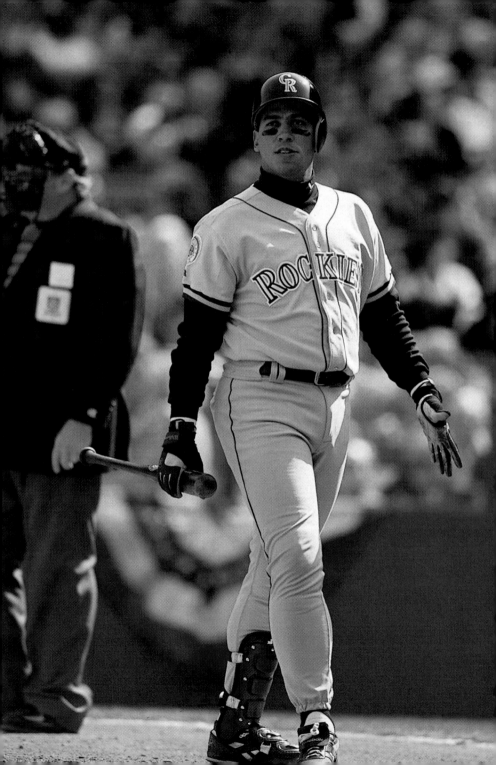

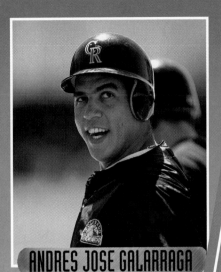

ANDRES JOSE GALARRAGA

ANDRES JOSE GALARRAGA

Date of Birth **June 18, 1961**

Height **6' 3"**

Weight **235 pounds**

Uniform Number **14**

Nickname **"The Big Cat"**

NL Gold Glove Winner **1989, 1990**

NL All-Star **1993**

Honor **Rockies all-time home-run leader**

★ MAJOR LEAGUE STATISTICS ★

Season	Team	AVG	H	HR	RBI
1985	Montreal	.186	14	2	4
1986	Montreal	.271	87	10	42
1987	Montreal	.304	168	13	90
1988	Montreal	.302	184	29	92
1989	Montreal	.257	147	23	85
1990	Montreal	.256	148	20	87
1991	Montreal	.218	82	9	33
1992	St. Louis	.243	79	10	39
1993	Colorado	.370*	174	22	98
1994	Colorado	.318	133	31	85
1995	Colorado	.279	155	31	106
1996	Colorado	.303	190	47*	150*
Totals (12 Seasons)		**.276**	**1561**	**247**	**911**

*Led League

ABOUT THE AUTHOR

Mark Stewart grew up in New York City in the 1960s and 1970s–when the Mets, Jets, and Knicks all had championship teams. As a child, Mark read everything about sports he could lay his hands on. Today, he is one of the busiest sportswriters around. Since 1990, he has written close to 500 sports stories for kids, including profiles on more than 200 athletes, past and present. A graduate of Duke University, Mark served as senior editor of *Racquet,* a national tennis magazine, and was managing editor of *Super News*, a sporting goods industry newspaper. He is the author of every Grolier All-Pro Biography and four titles in the Children's Press Sports Stars series.